T0381459

All

is

True

HELENNASTRI

authorHOUSE®

AuthorHouse™
1663 Liberty Drive
Bloomington, IN 47403
www.authorhouse.com
Phone: 833-262-8899

Published by AuthorHouse 02/06/2025

ISBN: 979-8-8230-4077-8 (sc)
ISBN: 979-8-8230-4076-1 (e)

Library of Congress Control Number: 2024927216

Print information available on the last page.

YES, I FOUGHT LIKE A GIRL...BUT I WON

I was at work and as usual I picked up the ringing phone expecting to hear a customer asking a question. Instead it was the surgeon from my doctor's office on the other line. "You have cancer", she said. It all seemed surreal when those words were spoken to me. Yet when I first found the lump I instantly knew it was indeed cancer.

Years ago I had a lumpectomy and I remember how the lump felt. No pain, no discomfort at all. It was shaped like a round ball. Small in size but neither the less intrusive. It didn't belong there. I immediately saw a specialist and he also suggested the removal. Surgery was arranged as a short procedure, I was in and out the same day. It was a done deal. The biopsy proved to be benign, and all was well.

This time I knew it was cancer. I had a mammogram a few weeks prior to finding this lump and the test showed no evidence of a growth or disease. Within a two week period, when I tried to lay on my stomach at bedtime, I couldn't. The pain, like a pinching, would prevent me from

3

sleeping in that position. I called my primary physician and made an immediate appointment.

During the examination, my doctor asked me what I thought of the lump. I answered quickly and calmly, "it's cancer." He responded saying, "why do you think this?" I answered, "because of it's shape and the discomfort from it". He looked down at the table and shook his head in agreement. From there my doctor sent me to a breast specialist at our local hospital. Keep in mind that this oddly shaped lump happened within a few short weeks of the mammogram.

I chose a female doctor, who was reportedly a brain at diagnostics and renowned for her excellent surgery skills. She thoroughly examined me and suggested a breast MRI. From this test she exclaimed that all doubts would be resolved. I was told to be patient that she would not have the results for about one week. She would call me with the results as soon as she received them. I returned to work and two days later I received her call. Yes, you have cancer. Come into my office so that I can show you on a chart where it is and how I will remove it.

I saw this doctor the next day. There was an open at her office and I grabbed it My daughter came with me to the appointment for moral support. The doctor laid out pictures of breast with cancer and showed me the one that best described where my cancer was and how my cancer spread into an area, she had hoped it didn't, but it did. She went on to say that it was an aggressive cancer, growing rapidly and had to be removed immediately. I agreed and arranged the surgery with her assistant and was to have it done in one week. Twelve days before Christmas. WOW.

The time of the surgery came quickly and for that I was glad. I wanted to feel better for the holidays as my two granddaughters, their husbands and one great grandson would be home for Christmas. Oh, and I can't forget the new puppy, who by the way became my best friend. The surgery went well and I felt really good, both mentally and physically. My surgeon placed a 24 hour pain pump in the operated breast and believe me, you did not feel pain. When it became emptied, you simply took eased the needle out and threw away it and the pump.

Two weeks home enjoying my family and back to work it was. The holidays were great but now it's time to see my surgeon and get a checkup. The surgical doctor told me that I would need chemo and some radiation and that she wanted me to meet my cancer team. I was in disbelieve because there was no previous indication by any doctor that further treatment would be necessary. I thought to myself, no, I will not get chemo or radiation.

The breast specialist then escorted my daughter and I to meet with the oncologist and radiologist, the doctors, to whom would be my cancer team. The radiologist exclaimed the radiation treatments and the length of time it was expected to take. Six weeks at five days per week. That's thirty shots of radiation. Yet the radiation treatments didn't scare me in the least. I at the time did not realize the dangers connected with radiation.

Then came my oncologist. What a surprise, my daughter worked with this doctor at a hospital years ago when she was a cancer nurse. He immediately recognized her and they greeted one another. He privately spoke with her before he came in the office to see me. My daughter, at my request was allowed in the room with me mostly because I knew she would understand all the medical terms and treatment offered. The oncologist introduced himself to me and then went on to describe the chemo and how I would be on four different drugs. He said it wouldn't be easy, he felt he had to go this route because of the cancer being aggressive. No, I wasn't mentally prepared for this part. Chemo treatment? Are you kidding? The cancer has been removed, just give me radiation and let me go on my way. My daughter could see the expression on my face and explained to me that this was all a part of getting well. No, I do not want further treatment and I am going to express how I feel.

I tried to explain clearly to the oncologist that I had a fatty and fibrous liver, and that I was fearful of further damage to it. I continued to tell the doctor that I had a liver biopsy and he should look at the results in my file before determining the chemo treatments. I had several MRI's of the liver through the past ten years saw a liver specialist, who can verify what I said. How foolish I must have appeared saying all those facts to this doctor, who surely looked over my entire file from the hospital. He was so patient with me and just let me go on and on.

My daughter was concerned about my emotional being and expressed her worry. I was honest with her when I said that I was angry. Not afraid, but very angry and she looked confused. I explained to her why I was angry. It was because my life was so busy with working, being the main salary, responsible with all the household duties, shopping, taking care of her dad, who suffered from COPD and so on. How could I possibly continue to do everything I do if after having the cancer removed and then be tied up with further needed treatment?

The oncologist continued to explain the why's of chemo and radiation but I was so filled with anger that his words were just insult after insult as far as I was concerned. My mind was in a turmoil, blank one second and these new facts running at a speed I never before experienced. I wanted to scream shut up, I don't want to hear this. The doctor tried to state that the chemo would not cause my liver to decline. He stated that he would carefully monitor my treatments and my liver enzymes to be sure that my liver function was not in jeopardy. This poor doctor continued on to try and convince me that I was in good hands and that the treatment would not harm my internal organs.

I saw myself getting angrier and told him that if he said one more bad thing I would slap him. Can you imagine yourself saying this to a doctor? In my right mind I would never be that disrespectful to a doctor or anyone else for that matter. When I said those horrible words, he didn't blink an eyelash. He looked at my daughter, who was totally embarrassed and then he simply tried to go over the facts with me again. When he saw my anger/anxiety continue to rise, he put the facts into shocking words. "If you don't accept the treatments I have laid out for you, you'll be dead in a few months". He continued on with, "your type of cancer is very aggressive, you have over a three stage cancer diagnosis and without treatment you have no chance of surviving." Well, that certainly shut me up. I then put my emotions aside and agreed to treatment, I was forced to face the true facts and accept my doctor's care. I wanted to live.

All this anger that poured out of me, I believe came from an inner fear that I refused to face. I truly believe I was not afraid of the cancer itself. My fear was the fear of not being able to continue to take care of things at home and work. More importantly, I feared for my family and how they would take this news. I was mom, Nan and GG. They could count on me. I was healthy, dependable, and strong and needed no help. I tried to help everyone where I could. I didn't want my family to worry about me. Their lives are ahead of them and I wanted their energies focused on their futures, not on my present.

Afraid of cancer...no I truly wasn't. I put myself in God's hands and His will. I knew I did not have control of this disease and from the day I found the growth, I accepted God's plan for me, whatever that was. This acceptance gave me peace and erased any fear I might have carried for myself. I just had a huge problem with being unable to carry on with my life's responsibilities. There were persons expecting my continuing role of being there for them and taking care of things. I worried more about them than myself. You know, super mom Mom, who loves them to the moon and back. My family is my life. My heart is there heart, now and forever.

The memory of surgery twelve days before Christmas still seems like a dream. A partial mastectomy was given and I was sent home the same day of surgery. The discomfort I had wasn't worth complaining about because of the pain pump. Before the chemo treatments began, I had to have a short procedure done to insert the portal in my chest. This way they could feed the chemo through this line each time I went for treatment. It avoids having to run a line in your veins each visit. The chemo treatments began, my daughter insisted on keeping me company. She made use of her time there by fussing over other cancer patients. They loved her. Eight hours sitting in the chair being fed the toxic drugs they use to 'cure' you. The first treatment was with the four chemo drugs plus a drug for nausea and one was steroids. Before I was sent home, they gave me a shot of white cells, a drug called Neurogen, and warned me that this medication will cause some pain. I would be receiving this shot after every chemo treatment. I went to work every day for about five weeks because the chemo went so well.

Another treatment and the white cell shot and still no vomiting, no uneasy pain, "hey, this isn't so bad". That feeling did not last too long. Within twenty four hours of that treatment I was in terrible pain. I was at work when the worse pain hit me. I wasn't able to focus and could barely walk. I called out to one of my co-workers to get me relief and painfully walked to my employer's office and announced to her that I couldn't be there any longer. That I needed to go on medical leave until my treatments were complete.

The pain increased and by the time I got home I was ready to pass out, my body was exhausted from holding on. It was hard to breathe because the pain traveled from my head to my toes. Thank God, I made it home. Later that day I noticed that I also broke out in hundreds of little blisters. They spread like wildfire, in my mouth, nose, all orifices and the bottom of my feet. It was painful to walk and sleeping was near impossible. My daughter called the oncologist PA and she called in a script to our pharmacy to help stop the blisters. Sh stated to my daughter that the pain I was having was from the white cell shot and the pain will decrease in a day or so.

The blisters in my mouth went away from the medication the PA prescribed, but my hands and feet weren't relieved. In fact the bottom of my feet would fill up with a fluid and harden so quickly into sheets that looked and felt like plastic that I would hear them crack as I tried to walk. I would sit on a chair and pee/ pieces of this human plastic off the bottom of my feet only to see that overnight this unusual occurrence would reappear. My hands looked like things from science fiction. My fingers would swell up and peel constantly. The skin didn't feel like skin but like a soft rubber. The rest of my body was swollen from my face to my toes. The steroids were the cause of the swelling. Last but not least I lost my hair. I was totally bald. I had my son take a picture of my baldness and I sent that picture through email to my family. On the picture I had a big smile and was pointing to my bald head.

Weeks went by and my treatments continued on but with one good outcome, my oncologist discontinued one of the four cancer drugs. The one the nurses called this the 'killer drug'. It was red and fed directly into your portal at the end of your regular chemo treatment. I felt a difference without that killer drug. I wasn't in as much pain and I slept most of the day without it in my system. My blisters also stopped appearing but the liquid in my feet that turned into what I named 'human plastic' continued on. But any improvement I saw and felt since the 'killer' drug wasn't in me was worth more than I can express.

Months went by and one day my oncologist approached me with good news. I believe you need only one more chemo treatment. He said he believed the cancer should be gone but to be sure he wanted me to have one more go at it. My daughter and I were elated by the news. The doctor said that even though I will have another chemo treatment, he wanted me to start the radiation schedule immediately. I of course agreed. I contacted the radiation department the next day to arrange when I must come in, etc.

My thoughts ran wild. Thank you God! Thank you Jesus! You have cleansed me from this disease and I am free of that deadly illness. Thank you, thank you, and thank you. I kept repeating those words. My Lord, my God, my All, You have given me another chance at being there for my family. My heart is full of love and gratitude to You my sovereign Lord. Thank you from my entire being. I always prayed at night and first thing in the morning, but after this experience, I added this to my daily prayers. "Thank you Lord for curing me of cancer, and thank You for taking this disease out of my body". This was my thank you prayer and also my protection prayer to my God. I was in His hands and His will I have accepted with my trust.

Since I no longer had the severe pain and the last chemo was given to me, I decided to go back too work. Well truthfully, my insurance company from work said they would not continue paying me the 60% salary, Short Term Disability allowed only a 12 week endurance, therefore back to work I went. My radiation treatments were given to me every morning at 7:30 am. I arranged an early appointment so that I could get to work on time. My feet still collected some liquid which turned into the 'human plastic' but I cracked and peeled it off and added soft insoles to my shoes. A few weeks after my last chemo treatment, the liquid in my hands and feet stopped. Oh what comfort I felt when my feet got back to normal. What I did notice later on was my toenails became thick and hard to trim. Even to this day several of my toenails are thick, yet my fingernails became very weak, they are not a smooth nail. Instead they have bulging creases that I have to file down and brush on an acrylic to keep them from cracking and splitting, and to make them look half decent I have faced the fact that I will never have nice fingernails. Ah, but it's so good to be alive and well again.

I am into my fifth week of radiation and I am getting burnt. I made up my mind to tell the doctor in charge that I will not be returning. I had so much discomfort that I had to apply a burn solution on myself every morning, at lunch time and in the evening. This meant at work I had to spend time in the ladies room, disrobing my blouse and bra in order to apply the treatment.

Th1S was an Inconvenience at work because I used most of my half hour lunch time to do this. The radiations doctor came in to see me after my treatment and announced that I would not have to come for the sixth week treatment. I looked at him and said straight out that I didn't intend to show up. He asked me why and I bitingly said to him, "didn't you notice that I am burnt?" He quietly responded by saying, "yes, that is why I am canceling the last week." I didn't say another word because I thought it useless to continue the conversation. I was just happy that this was the last day of radiation and him.

From this point on it was just a matter of setting up appointments with the surgeon and the oncologist. I was to see each of them every three months the first year. I did not arrange to see the radiologist as they requested because I could not see the purpose and I explained this to both of the above mentioned doctors. I felt they saved my life and showed compassion, the radiologist didn't. The exam times with him were, a quick look at me and then proceeded to type in the computer. End of examination. Six months pasted by since my last radiation treatment. The radiation doctor called me to say I needed to be seen by him. I said absolutely not, I won't make an appointment. I could not see the reason why. I explained that I do see my surgeon and oncologist on a regular basis and if they felt the necessity of me seeing him, they would have suggested this to me, and they did not. Therefore, I could not justify paying another fee if it was not necessary. I never heard from him again. Ah freedom, glorious freedom from treatments of any kind. Thank you, my Lord, my God, my All.

After my last chemo treatment I went to my oncologist office and asked if my portal could be removed. He looked at my records and agreed that it was okay. He then made the arrangements for a surgical team to set up the time and date for surgery. This was a final gift of freedom from the disease. The portal never gave me discomfort while it was in my chest and it fed my body the drugs needed to get well. It was just so wonderful to be rid of the instrument from my body When I look at the scar it left, I find it hard to believe that what I went through. Oh God, I am so grateful to be alive and well.

This story ends with happiness, peace and gratefulness. My message to you, who reads this caption of my life, is to be aware of your body and any changes you find. See your doctor and take care of what needs to be dealt with. Do not be afraid...give yourself to God...trust Him and your doctors to take care of you.

IT'S ALL ABOUT ROB
MY SON, MY FRIEND

I wake each day hoping to see him again, please Lord, just one more time.

To see his smile, to know if he is happy and healthy again. To hug him one more time. To be with me, if only for the moment. To reassure me that heaven is now his home.

But now I stand alone. I live alone. I now feel the aloneness that feared me all my life. I know his dying is true...his bed hasn't been slept in and his recliner is now filled with his blanket, pillow and his tablet. And yet, each morning I say "good morning, my son", I love you, and I miss you". Sadly at the end of the day I say "goodnight, my son, my sunshine,' I love you"

Instantly reality hits me and I gaze at his empty bed and his recliner. As I stand numbly by, I am once again reminded of how he was restricted to his chair because of his dialysis, 7 days @ 10 hours per day. His prison. His hurtful imprisoned sentence at home.

I question if my soul went with him. My body is frail and shaky from the emptiness I feel inside. He was my buddy and friend. We were able to share our views and not fear that we offended others, for we were both a bit outspoken. We were conscious of others' opinions and feelings. We favored many of the same TV shows and often would sit together in the kitchen and watch the news and a show while eating our dinners.

We would debate topics and always come to the conclusion that we were both right in our opinions. We believed that we were so much alike in our thinking, and we were smart enough to keep our opinions between the two of us.

The deep hurt I feel in losing him is that I lost one of my reasons to be alive. He was indeed my best friend, my confidant and trustee. Having no one to share my thoughts with places me in a nothingness zone. A twilight of some kind.

My God, I am lost in the whirlwind of existence. These feelings I have, no one needs or wants me to share. Feelings of loss because of someone's death is not the norm that others feel comfortable being exposed to. I try not to burden people with my feelings or seeing me in tears. This way I think they won't avoid me. No one wants to feel your pain.

I wake up during the night's sleep...trembling, fearful and crying. My son has died, and I am lost for this loss of him. I hurt inside and my mind screams out, NO, È4C), please tell me that my Rob isn't gone. Please let me see him in his bed, or his recliner, sound asleep and peaceful. My son, my son, I miss you terribly.

When I close my eyes tonight for sleep, please dearest Lord, grant me to take my last breath before dawn. Only then will I feel peace in your glory and love. I will be with my son and the many others from my family, who left in death to join you, our savior.

As I look back into my youthful years and remember my ten uncles and seven aunts, who combined, enriched me with forty-five cousins. Things were going on, and there was always someone having a get together. 'Family', so important to me and all of my family.

Both grandparents were first generation from Italy, therefore making me third. I loved hearing stories about my grandfather and grandmothers childhoods. My grandfather had five siblings, and he was the youngest, but that didn't excuse him from working to help his mother with expenses.

Can you imagine a six-year-old obligated to help support his family? His father died and each child was forced to work at any job to contribute to the family. He was Carmine, who boldly walked his small village until he found employment. A kind owner of a bakery who knew of his circumstances offered him to deliver bread to certain customers, (including his family), to sweep the bakery floor each day for a few coins, bread to eat, and if needed, a spot on the bakery floor to sleep. Can you Imagine to be this responsible at age six! What joy Carmine felt. He was so proud of his accomplishment. He remained working for this kind baker until he reached age eight. Each of his siblings obtained work and the family was able to maintain a step up from poverty. From age eight,

Carmein was hired as a sheepherder until his late teens. He saved every coin he could for his passage to America.

My grandmother was a lovely village girl, who had four siblings. Her name was Concetta. I grew up admiring her for her domestic abilities. A spectacular cook. She was beautiful and my grandfather fell in love with her the moment he first saw her. He had to court her properly, and that meant every time he went to see her, prior their meeting, they were heavily escorted by several of the family. He was expected to pay a dowry for a promise to wed her. Carmein did not want to wait years to honor this agreement so he decided to go to America to work and send dowry monies to Italy to Concettas father. Once the dowry was paid in full, Concettas father and mother decided when Carmein could come to Italy and take her to America, where they will wed.

Now to share my son, Robs' life. I married young. At nineteen I was married and had a child, a little girl., named KaranLee. I was told by specialists that I would not have another child. My main health problem involved autoimmune diseases. I was very fertile, but on a monthly basis I had tubal pregnancies, which I lost. For five years I was treated for this problem. A hysterectomy was advised but my gynecologist felt I was too young. Plus the fact he knew how much I wanted another child. Finally, after five years of treatment I had a normal pregnancy, but it was touch and go. I kept on bleeding to the point an abortion was suggested. I couldn't. It was against my religion and at five months I felt butterflies in my belly. I felt life, my son Robs' life.

Rob was born on his due date. A beautiful boy. Coal black hair, and dark brown eyes He was very Collecy. That was only the beginning of his problems. Rob had several allergies. He could not have a formula. I tried different milks such as goats. He could not digest them. I made up a home formula that my grandmother told me about while she was alive. He did well on it. In fact, he loved the flavor of vanilla. Mmnn, he would sound out, and happily keep drinking his bottle.

When it was time to start him on baby foods, he had to be fed one jar of the same food for a solid week, mark down the results and the following week try another. And so on, and so on. His health greatly improved through the first year and he seemed to be stronger and happier.

Robs sister, KaranLee, was six years older and she treated her brother as if he were her special doll. They were so close. He looked at her as his best friend because she always showed him love. She loved dressing him up in girl clothes or his dad's polo shirts and they would announce a show they wanted to perform for us. Adorable! We would clap and yell, hooray, hooray. How wonderful those years were. They played so well together and for them life was grand. Rob would get so excited when Karan would get home from school. He would run to her with a big smile on his face. He screamed Ka Ka as soon as she walked in the door. When she had homework, his sister would give him paper so that he could pretend that he was also doing schoolwork at the kitchen table.

As a child, Rob always had leg cramps. His doctor would exam him and reply that he had growing pains. This later proved to be Muscular Dystrophy. By the time Rob was diagnosed he was an adult and living on his own. Treatment was simply pain pills. I didn't know then if MD was genetic, but I also have MD, which wasn't diagnosed until my late 40's. The treatment suggested was the same...pain pills.

How happy Rob was with his toys and the riding horsey he got from his nanny at Christmas. He would spend hours with his little gas station and pretend he was fixing the cars. Or his three wheeled bicycle that he would put his stuffed animals on to give them a ride. His happiest time was when his sister would come home from school. He would smile ear to ear, and scream Ka Ka, when she appeared at the door. Rob would be instantly re-energized just seeing her. They both missed one another so much. Those years of watching them grow and being so close could only make a parent thankful and blessed by God. There were so many happy years with Karan and Rob. I felt blessed to be their mother. Thank you, Jesus, I would say to myself. And when they would ask for a mommy hug, that was the greatest experience any mother could desire. Kisses, kisses and more kisses, with a giant hug and more kisses. Those were my happy days.

What a joy Rob was. He loved to see how things worked. Happy were his days when he had something to do with things that he could take apart and see how they moved or made a noise. Rob's imagination was so advanced that by the age of ten, we purchased a home computer for him. The salesman, who helped us with which one to purchase, claimed the computer memory, 16K, would last for several years. He told us Rob would have two to three years of usage before having to invest in a larger system. Within nine months we had to obtain more memory. From computer books, Rob was teaching himself how to code and design programs. Rob was happiest when his mind was at work and learning.

Rob was smart and wanted to be able to make money to buy things he wanted that his allowance couldn't afford. He became a paper boy at nine and he was so liked by his customers that he was tipped on a regular basis. When it rained he put each persons paper in a plastic bag and sealed it shut. He also made sure that he delivered his customers paper to their front door. He was very mannerly and always wished them a good day. People were impressed by his courteous and pleasant expressions. If you ask him why he made so much in tips, he would smile and remark that it is because he treats his customer with a smile and respect.

Rob was so proud of his income and proposed that he and I should have time together every Saturday and he would treat me to a soft pretzel and Italian ice. He insisted that I do not try and pay for our treat. After all, it was his treat, not mine. We would walk thru the mall and stop in the main shop, look around, stop to ponder on an item, either something I was interested or himself. He was so absorbed asking questions of the sales person that he impressed them to the point he had their attention and would get a discount on his purchase. The sales people knew his name and would always say hello. To me, they would praise Robs character and manners.

School was a bit disappointing to him. He needed to think on the subject the teacher was engaging and expand on it and then go further by asking many questions of the instructor. His mind was hungry to learn and know why, how, and when. He went to college and many days would be asked to teach the class. The professors fed him the challenge he needed and rewarded him by his teaching the class. Rob ended college with two associate degrees, a bachelor's degree, and a master's degree. He was also a member of Manses. Rob was a loner. He did not enjoy hanging in corners just to hang out. He often had friends over and they would be on the computer system playing games or watching their favorite teen shows. Robs best friend was Chris. The two of them hung together. They were pals.

Only once did Rob get into trouble. One of his friends got his first car. He called Rob and asked him to come and help him with putting in a system to self-start the car when it's cold., Rob agreed and went to help him. Rob loved working on anything that took thinking. The problem came when he asked his friend if he could drift his car to the corner. Nothing was parked in front of the car so his friend said yes. Rob did not drive yet and when he went to go forward...He went backward and hit a car close behind him. That was a $350.00 mistake which Rob had to pay. And he paid back every cent. Rob took a job as bus boy in a local burger place, and every paycheck was handed over to his friend until the entire bill was paid in full.

I would tease Rob about all the girls who wanted to go steady with him and he would seriously remark, "they want to get married, I don't". "1 am working on developing my own company and that will take most of my time, "he would say. His idea was to do private business programs that will completely operate a company's business, including their payroll, expediting shipping, deliveries and keeping record of sales and updates, taxes and employee records., and so on. His intentions were to develop and advertise his company before he finished college, so that he could pay for college... and he did just that. His company name was "Nastri Software Systems, LLC

Nearing graduation Rob updated his customers' company programs to an extended year so that they would have time to find other resources. Rob suggested three computer engineers, who Rob went over the details of each firm's programs, and they were hired by these businesses. Life seemed to be going Robs way. He graduated from college and looked forward to his future being an entrepreneur as a program engineer in computer science and design. Karan Lee, our daughter, was Rob's best friend. He felt the same towards her. She was married and later had twin girls Their names were Candace Leigh and Helennastri Renae.

Rob fell in love with them. He babysat often, giving his sister and her husband time to have a date or to just relax at home. As the girls grew up and began school, Rob would sit down with them and teach them math and the work of computers. He was devoted to the girls and loved them so dearly he would remark that he felt they were his daughters too. He supplied his nieces, Helennastri and Candace with their own personal computers and loaded them up with the latest programs. The girls idolized him and always wanted to be with him. They would play board games with no breaks and a deep desire to win against their uncle Rob. Monopoly was one of their favorites. Seven hours one Sunday at the kitchen table, and they wanted to play more. They also loved to have pillow fights with Rob.

Later, Rob met and fell in love with Ann Marie. They met in the field of business meetings. He said they had so much in common. From comparison of other woman, he dated, I sensed that he really loved her. They did everything together. Theater, movies, dinners, travel, boating and just hanging around. I was so happy for him. He was on a cloud of serenity. Sixteen years together. Holidays were special because Rob, Ann Marie, Al (Karan's husband), and his parents and both granddaughters and nephew, Dale came to dinner. After dinner we played board games. It was a night filled with laughter and munching on snacks.

Health problems became a nightmare for Rob and us. He had heart surgery because of CHF (Congestive Heart Failure), and high blood pressure, both of which were genetic curses from his father's side of the family. On my side was diabetes and cancer. Sounds as if there was no chance for a long life. Even with the proper care the sentence was given. The restrictions to take care of yourself to live a decent life were do able, but again, restricted. Life goes on and dreams develop but his health was tipsy curvy. This alone made him commit to NO children. He continued to love his nieces and spoil them.

He and AnnMarie continued to travel and enjoy life...just the two of them. They both worked hard and earned promotions and pay wages. I think sometimes when we are at the happiest, we can reach, and something bad has to happen to change our lives. Whether it be to help us grow or learn the hard way so that we learn a lesson needed. When he was first diagnosed with kidney failure, they never told us he would never be eligible for a kidney transplant. They had hoped to see he would improve with dialysis. But it really was already to late for his body to heal. They knew that his time was limited. They in fact were very sure he wouldn't make it to get a Kidney donor. Rob knew this but never told me or anyone else. He just wanted to be with family and try to enjoy the little time left that he knew he had.

Rob's health began to decline. He began to get worse with one infection after another, lymphedema got so severe, it caused weekly trips to the specialist to peel his legs and medicate them. Within a few months, Robs legs cleared up. We were so happy that this led us to believe that Rob was indeed getting better. Later we realized this wasn't the case. Rob was indeed very ill and he kept it a secret...to protect us. He wanted nothing more but to save us the pain of seeing him decline. We were never told that eventually his kidneys would worsen that he was gone too far in his condition to be on a kidney recipient list. The transplant doctor told Rob that he will not be a recipient for a kidney transplant because his body would not survive the surgery. They gave us no help in finding him refuge in the latest kidney treatment. Hope was out of the question, and he was fully aware of his condition and again he kept it from us.

His sister, Karan wanted to be on the donators list for Rob. I also wanted to be considered but I was told that I couldn't be a candidate for Rob for I had cancer 3 times. Rob silently confessed to me that he didn't want his sister to be a candidate. He felt she wasn't strong enough to pull through and the fact her husband needed her, because his health wasn't good. Plus, they just acquired a single home and were in the process of having remodeling work done on their home before they moved in.

My heart broke a bit more each day knowing that he wasn't going to get completely well. I was on the belief that Rob would be sickly the rest of his life. He dit not want the neighbors to know how he was. When he would join me on the patio with neighbors, he would put on a happy face to fake everyone out. Rob told me that he did not want our neighbors and family to think of him as my sick son.

I had already been a widow of one year and welcomed Rob to live with me. We always respected one another's privacy and promised to continue on getting him well enough to enjoy life again. Our first year of living together, Rob's health seemed to be going as the specialist hoped it would. Rob and I set up a room with shelves for his Comic Collection and the Comic Heroes Statues. All of which was his dream to continue his part-time business online. We set up his bedroom to accommodate the dialysis machine next to his recliner chair and his big screen TV for him to enjoy.

Rob seemed to be doing well health wise and he even started to cook meals. He loved to cook and

I enjoyed his cooking because he was really good at it. Rob continued to see his specialist one day each week. They did blood work weekly to make sure his condition was either improving but not getting worse., and to make sure he was following the procedures they agreed on. That first year went exceedingly well. Rob seemed happy and content, which was so important to me and our family.

The second year living with me, Rob's health began to decline. He began to get worse with one infection after another, I was never told that eventually his kidneys would take his life. I would have been in disbelief if told this, and I would have been driving the doctor crazy searching for any new medicines and treatments that were out there. They gave us no help in finding him refuge or hope. Two years later, toward his life ending, Rob's condition continued to worsen. He was always in pain, and the pain worsened. One day Rob blurted out "This isn't life, mom. I just want the Lord to take me". He spoke with his kidney specialists, and it was agreed to stop treatment. They explained that as of that day, there was not any treatment to make his health improve in the slightest.

They continued and went along with his dialysis treatment. They figured and hoped that dialysis would give him time to get somewhat better. At first, we thought it did, only because he hid his suffering. He hid his pain so that we would see him smile and enjoy seeing family and neighbors. But he couldn't hang on. His internal pain worsened, and he purchased pain pills and ate them like candy. He never complained, he would sit quietly and endure the pain. There was nothing for us to do but cringe in sorrow and plead to God to help him. At night, I would lay in bed crying silently while listening to his suffering below me, for his bedroom was on the first floor and I on the second.

Rob asked me and his sister Karan permission to stop dialysis. He claimed he was told that it would give him anywhere from two weeks to two years of life to live free of being on the machine for 10 hours per day, seven days a week. Within two weeks of not doing the treatments, my son, Rob passed away. He died sitting in his favorite recliner in his bedroom. I later learned that he was never told that he may be alive without dialysis. The truth was he would die within a day, a week, or two weeks, not more.

Knowing that he was suffering so much. I would not leave him alone. The night before he passed away, I lay in his bed, Rob was on his recliner which was moved right next to the bed. I held his hand all night. I didn't want him to be alone one second. We slept through the night. I woke up very early and just laid there holding his hand. He opened his eyes and just looked at me. He tried to smile and when I noticed this, I asked him if there was anything I could do, He nodded no and half smiled.

I told him I loved him dearly and he blinked his eyes. I lay there holding his hand filled with fear knowing that I was losing my son. I realized I knew...but did not want to admit it. I don't want my son to die. I did not want to know that he was already dying. The pain he felt was his body slowly dying. I was never told what others knew. It was unfair of me to expect my family to tell me the truth. After all, they were also in pain with the thought of loosing. Him.

The second day of May, at 3:48 pm, My son took his last breath. My daughter, Karan heard his last breath, and I screamed hysterically as I went to him. I knelt down and put my hands out to him and I held his face in my hands and cried deeply. 'No, No, No. Please God don't let this happen. Rob then pulled himself up and desperately blurted to me,' I love you.' I laid my head on his chest, looking up at him and begging him not to die. I put a finger on each of his eyelids and moved them hoping to see life. I only saw his eyes staring at me...with no feeling. I screamed 'No, no, please don't die. I promise I will always take care of you. I will never leave you.' Oh God, No don't take my son.

Looking back, I know that I was in denial. People who were our friends knew that I didn't want to face the facts of his condition. I made myself believe that his treatments were healing him to the point that although he would never be fully healthy again, he would outlive me. I told myself that when I passed on, his sister, Karan would take care of him. And he would always have AnnMarie coming by to spend time with him. They were still in love and that made me happy. Life can be very cruel, hard and unforgiven.

And now I am alone again. I was left to cry with my bleeding-heart memories. My son is gone... forever gone. His room is empty of him, and I am empty without him. Please God, let me die too. This is too painful! please let me die, let me die, I want to die. I found myself making deals with God. Take my house, my car, all monies I managed to save...please take it all, just please leave my son with me, alive.

I do try to be optimistic and smile when my neighbors or friends are around me.

Especially when my family is visiting or calling by phone, I still cry, and I admit I do not like my life anymore. In fact, when Rob first passed away,

I begged God to take me. To please take away my breath and end my nightmare. Here I am eleven months later, alone again. The Lord, Jesus knows my future, where or when I die is ip his hands. I trust and love my God. Therefore, I still exist, with a hole in my heart and an emptiness in my entire being.

Each day I struggle to get through the day by keeping busy. I admit I hate being alone. No one to share a day's thoughts or a meal. Friends and family cannot fill the hole in my stomach. They cannot heal my torn heart. Each of them suggests that I get a pet. They don't understand that yes, a pet gives lots of love, but they can't fill the emptiness inside of me. I do not feel I am ready to take their advice and get a pet. It wouldn't be fair to the pet. Maybe next Spring. We'll see.

My late uncle Rudy once said that a parent should never outlive their child. It is the worst pain that a parent will ever feel. My cousin Cheryl went thru that pain after her daughter died. My niece Debra lost a daughter, and other members in my

family lost a child. Each of them said the same...
'It's the most painful experience a parent could go
through.'

I can't believe how fast the months have passed.
The holidays are near and I don't care. Christmas
is next week...l am trying my best to be silent
about how horrible I feel. I am alone...why don't
they understand and at best don't suggest I move.
To move this soon would only make things worse
for me. So many memories to deal with...so many
feelings that still deeply hurt me inside. It is so
hard to face my days without my son. He was my
strength and comfort because I wasn't alone. I
sometimes think that lam being punished, that
being alone is my curse., my hell on earth.

My eightieth birthday is this month, January
22, I will be taken to dinner in center city by my
granddaughter, Carmella and her husband Chris
with their daughter Autumn, and my daughter,
Karan and her husband Al, and daughter Candace
and her son Kyle. Karan ordered a picture on
canvas of Rob and Karan together. I believe their

ages were, Karan age 16 and Rob age 10. Can't wait to see it and hang it up in my home. I look forward to the dinner and greatly appreciate my family for caring so much. It will make them happy to know they made my birthday a happy occasion. I love them dearly and appreciate them. They are a happy part of my life. I don't see them often, maybe once a month, they have their lives and responsibilities, only fair to them for me not to be demanding. I am blessed to have such a wonderful family. I love them dearly, and I am thankful that they are in my life and show their love.

Dinner downtown was great, I really enjoyed myself and the food was just like my grandmother prepared when she was alive. She had 17 children. 10 sons, (all of whom served our country) and 7 daughters who ruled the house alongside my grandmother. My grandparents, Carmien and Concetta were greatly admired and respected in their town, Shamokin, Pa. There were often times the newspaper had a long article about them and the 10 sons, who were raised to respect others and work hard. Shamikin, Pa, is in central, west of Pa. A small town that in its early days was one of the best coal mining towns. By the time I was a teenager, most coal mines were closed. For decent employment, people had to travel to Harrisburg, Pa, which was an hour's ride from Shamokin.

I remember the year my uncle Dante died. He was only 18. He came home for Christmas and on his return, his plane crashed. The plane crashed into the quicksand of Louisiana. His body was never recovered (which my grandmother, did not know). The coffin was sealed and emptied of Dante's body. Two soldiers, one each side of his coffin, stood guard so no one went near his coffin. My Nan cried every day for her Dante. She shed her last tears when she passed away.

My son and daughter loved hearing memories about their great grandparents, and I loved telling them. After all those stories were a part of our history, and my son and daughter were in awe learning about the old country and how their families lived in poverty with dignity and honor. To the end of their lives, they lived with honesty and love of God. In fact, the mayor of Shamokin presented them with the keys to the city and a plaque stating that they were honorable and generous citizens. I was so honored to be an extension of themselves, and I truly tried to be an example and share with my two children the love for our country and the devoted family we stem from.

This story is about my son, Robert. He was not only a good son and brother, and uncle, he was love to all of his family.

My two granddaughters, Helennastri and Candace were the second stream of my happiness. They lived two twin homes from me and on the same side of the street. When they were tiny tots, and thru most of their teens, they were at my house every day. We played games, sang songs and they used my personal computer to draw, write songs or just to be silly. I have called them my angels since they were born. I wrote poems about them and all my thoughts of them I record and put them in the computer for the future.

Before I die, I will give each of them a folder of what I wrote. I am sure that will give them pleasure that perhaps they will read to their children. My angels gave me years of happiness and joy.

If Rob were alive, I am sure he would be happy to share his time with the girls. He and I often talked about them and the fun we had with them in our lives. Rob and AnnMarie never had children, but they enjoyed the girls immensely. They met in their forties and decided that having children at the ages of late forties wasn't a good idea. So they grabbed the experience of parenthood through nieces and nephews. To me that was so brave and unselfish because they both loved children.

This is life...You don't get everything you want; therefore, you make life as good as you can.

Dear Rob,

MaMa loves you and misses you with every breath I take. My heart is your heart now and forever.

RALPH
THE GENTLE GIANT

Ralph was the young boy and the grown man, who loved animals. He had three dogs, several horses and two white peacocks, named Romeo and Juliet. He treasured these creatures and cared for them, as his children.

Ralph loved spending time fishing on his small boat. He enjoyed the beauty of God's earth and the quiet of the day. Ralph embraced the peacefulness of solitude.

His tender heart and giving nature, touched everyone who knew him. He never complained.

He never made demands. Ralph simply accepted life's circumstances and went on living.

His large hazel eyes and his childlike smile melted your heart. You wanted desperately to ensure his needs and happiness. He was shy, for he was as his mother.

Innocence, vulnerability. Hushed emotions... all was Ralph.

Gratefulness, loss of words and a shy glance... those were Ralph.

Ralph was a son, a brother, a brother-in-law, an uncle, a great grand uncle, a cousin, a nephew and everyone's friend.

Ralph truly was love...lets celebrate his life.

Ralphs Epitaph...May 2007.

Who could have known that his life would be so hard. Along with his special needs, he felt unwanted by his father, despaired and helpless with his sickly mother and alone, very alone.

I remember the day my mother brought Ralph home from the hospital. He was so beautiful. His large hazel eyes with eyelashes that every girl wants for herself. And his smile was intoxicating. You couldn't resist kissing him. There was a problem though, Ralph's legs were set in casts. I was first upset to see this and quickly asked my mother why and she calmly answered that the caste were put on his legs so that would grow straight. Poor little Ralph lying there with those heavy casts. He couldn't turn or kick his feet. Yet he was smiling all the time. His magnificent eyes would stare at you pleading, "please love me l" and his smile was to let you know that he already loved you. How could you refuse loving him.

I recall Ralph that first year going through the stages, newborns do and he seemed to be a happy baby, even though he was restricted in movement. Our mother was devoted to him. She lovingly saw to his every need and constantly kissed and caressed him.

It was celebration time when the doctors took the casts off his legs. I vaguely remember his age. He must have been seven or eight months old when that occurred. He was sitting up himself and he was beginning to get around in his wheeled seat. Happiness engulfed our home because Ralph had such a delightful disposition. I loved making him laugh. I loved my baby brother.

Ralph wasn't quite a year old when the seizures began. No warning from the doctors, who saw him on a regular basis. I suppose back then, (in the early 50's) they couldn't know what expect or they would have prepared my mother. I remember Ralphs first seizure. His eyes rolled to the back of his head and his body shook feverishly. It was a nightmarish experience. I screamed and cried hysterically as did my mother.

Thank God, Ralph's father kept calm and took over to make sure Ralph was not choking on his own tongue. He kept saying while hugging our mother that he will be alright and not to worry. Within seconds it was over. At the time of Ralphs seizure it seemed such a long time, endless and frightening.

Ralph continued to have seizures of this type until he was a toddler. As he grew into his school years his seizures changed to silent ones. I believe they are called grand mall. You knew when they were happening because Ralph would be playing one minute and the next minute he would just stare until the seizure was over.

Growing up for Ralph was difficult. He was slower than other children. The seizures apparently did damage. Even so Ralph had to go to school. He needed extra help in learning and this put a physical strain on our mother. Mom was devoted in helping Ralph learn the basics. After years of persistence, moms hard work paid off. Ralph learned the basics of reading and writing and even arithmetic. He hated school and repeated grades from 1 thru 4ᵗ' By then he was thirteen and had Enough, he ran away from home.

Mom's health wasn't good. This stemmed from childhood. As a young girl of seven years, she developed whooping cough, which in her day was fatal in most cases. She nearly died and was left without the ability to talk and walk. This was an extreme burden for my grandmother during this time. Grandmother had eight of her twenty children, (seventeen survived), left to raise.

My grandmother said it took two years for mom to relearn both walking and talking. Her childhood sickness caused her to always be with health problems. She was left with a weak heart, which brought many ill health issues to her frail body. Her medical history had many doctors shake their heads in wonder how she was still existing. She was left with a weak heart at a very young age, but that was only one of her health issues.

Moms health continued to decline during her teen and adult life. She did attend school but only to the sixth grade. This left her to be at home helping her mother raise the brothers and sisters that were born after her. All the older children had a roll to play in aiding this large family. The older boys sold produce door to door and the girls had to help with the younger children. The story of their life raising such a large family, you can only imagine the trials and tribulations they encountered, is heart rendering and must be told at a later time.

I remember my mom in the hospital at least twice a year. She became diabetic and developed thrombosis. The thrombosis caused blood clots to burst with the slightest bump.

I can still see clearly the times this happened and how the blood would just spray out of one of her legs would get panicky, crying and begging someone to help as I was running for a neighbor. The neighbors always assisted and saw that mom was taken to the emergency room. The attending physicians always had to keep her, sometimes for days, weeks, depending on the condition she was in.

There was this time when a blood clot was traveling to her heart and lungs. Surgery was an absolute necessity. The family was notified that mom may not make it through the surgery but there was no choice,. If they didn't operate she would definitely die. At least she would have a chance if the doctors could successfully get the clot out.

The family was notified that mom may not make it and they packed up, came to the city to be with mom. They filled two waiting rooms and prayed during moms surgery. Praise God, mom made it and the family filled the room with praises and thanks to God.

A long recuperation was at hand. Two of mom's sisters stayed on at our house to clean and cook and take care of mom. Another critical hospital stay was when mom got a blister on her foot. Being a diabetic caused her foot to be badly infected and they had to remove part of the foot. This visit in the hospital took several weeks. She stayed with me for her care and recovery. Later that year, a serious infection took hold of the same leg and into the hospital she went. The infection took on gangrene and the doctors believed her leg had to be amputated. Again the family was notified and several came to be with her at the hospital. My aunt Gloria had sent away to Spain for the blessed water from the Lourdes fountain. Gloria wiped the blessed water all over my moms leg and foot. We prayed and gave our pain to God for the fear that my mom would die.

The doctors came to us with news that they couldn't explain...the gangrene was gone. They were bewildered with their findings. She did not have gangrene and would be watched for two more weeks. The gangrene never came back. It was extremely important for me to help mom with housework, errands and cooking the meals.

Taking care of Ralph became a game for him. I wanted him to help with little things for mom so that he felt important. He was in charge of her.

He was to be her checker player, get her a drink, get the mail and hand it to her, answer the phone and finally make her smile. And I was Ralphs fill in mother.

I sometimes lost my patience with Ralph. He would run from me. Sometimes hide when you were calling for him to do homework, or it was dinner time and he knew I would ask him to wash up, and at bedtime he would hide because he didn't want to go to bed. Occasionally I had to slap him and when I would look at him and those big hazel eyes, I pitied him and couldn't stay mad and I would beg him to be good and I would cry. I couldn't stay mad at him and he knew it. He would give me a smile that was irresistible. And I resist him. I had to be the one who had to be strong, after all I was his only defense with the outside world. I loved him so and I knew hoe much he loved me.

When we were watching TV at night, Ralph would cuddle up to me. We loved to watch scary movies and the oldie comics with Jerry Lewis, (who Ralph imitated). Most evenings when mom wasn't sick, mom, Ralph and I would watch Fred Astair, Jeannette McDonald and Ginger Rodgers, and moms favorite, Shirley Temple. Mom should watch Shirley Temple over and over again and still cry when Shirley was in trouble. Ralph and I would laugh hysterically.

Ralph's father was not mine. He, Emile and my mother married when I was five. Mom became pregnant and had Ralph when I turned six years of age. In the first years of their marriage, Emile was a good father to me. As I grew up and my mothers health declined Emiles disposition became filled with resentment and anger and I was his target. Back in those days Medical insurance was only for the above middle class. Imagine how the expenses accumulated with all the hospital stays my mother continued to have. Desperation and despair and the lack of steady work burdened my stepfather and he saw no help in getting work. His depression and anger grew.

Emile told me that he can't even look at me without dislike. Ralph during this period was still at a young age where his father could still tolerate him, after all Ralph was his son. Emiles anger turned into violence and too many times I felt his wrath. I was 15 and I couldn't take his threats or abuse. Or the fact that he laid in my bed while I was sleeping. I sensed him there and jumped up and over him. I ran to my neighbor next door and stayed there until I heard him leave to look for work.

I took my brother to our aunt Beatrice's and asked her to contact mom at the hospital, letting her know that we were staying with her for a visit. To our surprise mom was being released the next day. After talking to her sister, my mother called her parents upstate and asked them to come and get me and Ralph. Two uncles and an aunt. My grandparents wanted Ralph and I to live with them and they offered my mom to come home. She explained she couldn't because of her doctors and treatments she was having. At least that was the excuse she gave them. Ralph had to stay behind because his father refused to let him go. "He's my kid and he is staying here". My grandparents had no choice but to leave him. My uncles and aunt pleaded with my stepfather to let Ralph come with them. They promised the would be treated good and loved. They tried to impress Emile with not having Ralph as a responsibility the pressure for Emile would be lessened a great deal for him.

My poor mother, sick and weak from being in the hospital, stood crying helplessly. Her heart was broken but she sacrificed herself to give me a chance of living a safe live without violence.

Kneeling in the back seat and looking out the window at my mother and my poor brother, I cried helplessly. I prayed, Please God don't let anything happen to them. Protect Ralph from his fathers anger and have cousin Jim visit him more. Jim could always make Ralph smile and feel safe. They'll go fishing and to the stables. Jim knows how to calm Ralph down. Ralph hid from company he didn't know. His shyness and mistreatment from his peers compelled him to be fearful of most people. Oh God, who is going to protect my poor brother while 1m, gone. Jim can't be with him all of the time. I cried at the thought of something happening to him.

I lived with my grandparents during the school year and came home for the summer months. Ralph was elated that I was home again. We sat up late watching TV and ate our favorite snacks that mom had gotten for us. Ralph kept saying how happy he was that I came home. When asked how Ralph became his old silly self again. The house was filled with laughter and not a quarrel occurred often I had a few girlfriends over and Ralph was always included. My girlfriends were great with Ralph.

Mom took ill again. Her Thrombosis caused veins to burst again she was admitted into the hospital. They had to keep her to be sure no blood clots were traveling through her system. Slowly I saw the change in Emile. He was quieter. He would discard his tools anywhere but where they should go. He would leave his dirty clothes anywhere and instead of eating what dinner I prepared, he would make something else. Bad signs. I knew if mom wasn't home soon to be released from the hospital, her husband would go right back to being rambunctious. I told Ralph that if and when his father carried on, that he should run and hide. If things got really bad, that he should run to a neighbors house. Our neighbors knew how things would get in our house and they surly would help protect Ralph.

One day Ralph went to play with some of the neighborhood kids and I went to call him in for lunch and couldn't find him. None of the kids knew where he was. I first looked into our back alley way but saw no sign of him at this end of the block. I continued down our street block so I could check that ends ally way. I walked thru the ally to the other end, and when I reached it, I didn't realize what I was seeing at first. Someone was laying in the alley with his arms covering his face. My girlfriend Phyliss lived nears and joined me to check this person. Oh my God, it's Ralph and he is covered in blood. I screamed in panic and fear that he might be dead. Phyliss and I went to him and he was crying. Just laying there covered in blood and crying. I checked him to see where the blood was coming from and I asked him, who did this to you, I asked, but he only cried. Phyliss and I each took and end of his body and carried him to our house.

We laid Ralph on the couch and I washed the blood off his face and his body. He was beaten up. His face was bruised from the punches he sustained and the blood was from his nose and mouth. Again I asked him who did this to you. This time he gave me the name. NEAL.

Phyliss and I ran to Neal's houses which was right next door to hers and I banged on his door. I screamed for Neal to come out. His mother came to the door and warned me not to touch her son. Neal peaked out the door Phjyliss and I warned him to be afraid to come out because we were going to beat the shit out of him. Neal was older than Ralph and was a bully to all the younger kids. His mother did nothing to correct her son so his bullying got worse for the other kids...not for Ralph.

How come...l beat the crap out of Neal. He never bullied Ralph again.

Our cousin Jim, who was Ralph's age would come and stay on weekends. Jim and Ralph were best friends. They would spend hours fishing one day and the other day at the stables. Both boys loved nature. They liked to hike and explore. When they were together all you would hear is laughter. Jim was so good for Ralph. Jim was shy but did not have special needs. His shyness made him understand Ralph like no other person. Jim was also protective of Ralph. He would not let anyone hurt Ralph and his warning to them would only be made once.

Jim and Ralph were so happy together. Life to them was a circus. They both loved animals and not being in school. It was summer and that is their fun time. Swimming, fishing, the stables and just roam around and enjoy life the best they can.

My summer being home with Ralph and my mother was ending. I had to back upstate with my grandparents for school. I hated to leave my mother and brother. Ralph knew I'd be home for Christmas so he took my leaving in stride.

To me, Christmas seemed so far away Will they be alright. Will mom get sick again. Phyliss and her brother said they would protect Ralph. I really wasn't worried about Neal. Neal definitely took friend Phyliss's threat serious. Then there is cousin Jim. Until school starts he will be sure to look after Ralph.

The day came and an uncle came to pick me up. It is a three hour journey so my uncle was staying overnight so he could be rested for tomorrows trip. Saying goodbye was hard. I remember looking at Ralph and by his smile I could see that he didn't realize I would be gone for so long a time. My poor brother, he is so innocent, so not aware of what is going on. I could only hope that threats I put out to those few rough kids would be taken seriously and they would do Ralph no harm.

Every time mom would call me I would ask her about Ralph. Mom would give me the scoop and I was rest assured that things were okay with Ralph. I needed to know that the both of them were good.

It is the only way I could stay at my grandparents the winter months.

After returning to my grandparents, I was introduced to two weeks of canning tomatoes and vegetables with my grandmother and two aunts. Dozens of shelves were filled with jars of whole tomatoes, crushed tomatoes, and a variety of vegetables for the winter months. They also prepared dozens of jars filled with different fruit preserves for bread and toast and whole fruits to enjoy during My grandmother also made Creme Dementhe. She also made Anisette liquor. Both of her drinks were expert in taste.

My grandfather made his famous deep red wine. He was known in several counties for the best wine, made with no sugar. People came from several counties to visit pop and mom and get to taste his wine and be given a quart to take home and enjoy. In the cellar you would find several shelves filled with jars of canning goods and 3 Barrels of the best wine in Pennsylvania. People from several counties would visit my grandparents and share in the reward of canned goods and great wine as a gift from them I spoke with my mother once a month by phone and weekly by letter. During one conversation she began to cry saying Ralph disappeared a few weeks ago. After struggling to get my mother to say if she knew where he was, she grasped and said yes, that he was living at the stables. Ralph was only eleven years old at the time. He would hide on the stable grounds into the barns when the owner closed his horse rental business.

After mom found out where he was, (through cousin Jim), she went to the stables and confronted the owner. He turned out to be a very nice man and ultra concerned for Ralph. He understood that Ralph was extremely unhappy because of his father. It took him weeks to get Ralph to trust him enough t o When our mom was in the hospital and I was upstate, Ralph felt he had no one to defend him, so he ran away to the only place where he felt he could be safe. Ralphs utopia was at the stables with all of the horses. He was at home there and was treated well.

Ralph cleaned the barns, fed and brushed the horses for a place to stay. It was an agreement that the owner and Ralph made together. The communication between mom and the owner of the stables gave mom a sense of security on Ralph's wellness.

As usual I came home after school let out. I graduated from high school and was expected to return to Philadelphia to live with my mother and to find employment. The house was in dyer need of heavy cleaning and was my first priority. After two solid weeks scrubbing and rearranging closets, drawers and furniture pieces, the house started to look decent again.

It wasn't the same this time home. Ralph wasn't here. He had been gone over a year. Mom said she went to the stable to see him and was told that he left for a ranch somewhere in Jersey. She was beside herself and didn't know where to begin to locate him. All the owner knew was that Ralph with good people and he was safe there.

Later that summer Ralph called our mother. She cried and begged him to come home and promised him things would be better. Ralph said no, that he was happy where he was and would not come home. Mom convinced Ralph to give her the names of the ranch and owners. Ralph and mom both agreed to keep in touch. This was enough for my mother to keep her sanity.

Mom called Ralph a few times a month. Mom even got to speak with the owners of the ranch and they convinced her that they loved Ralph and would see to it that he was taken care of. Ralph was with this ranch family for twenty odd years. He earned his room and board by taking care of the horses and stables and whatever odd jobs needed tending. He was able to go fishing, attend rodeos, go to horse auctions and enjoy the outdoors. He swore this life made him happy.

Later that year I got married and had a child, a little girl. She was a gift of God. My mother was in her glory. As my daughter got older, she spent a few weeks with my mother during the summer months. Cousins at my age group spent the entire summer with our grandmother. We had Shamokins mountains to climb, The unused pig pens to play cowboy and indians, the parked railroad cabooses to play in and our attic at our grandmothers that was made into our private house, filled with games and trains, boats to become captain in and our vivid imaginations to play out a story.

What a beautiful time at our grandparents we had. On Saturdays our grandmother would get the small brown paper bags from their store and fill each one with all kinds of fruit for us to eat at the movie. Every Saturday was cartoon day and grand mom would treat us to the movies. So we would have the bag of great fruit and a quarter to pay for the show. We would sit in the first row and when the movies began and the crowd would start to scream and clap, all of us cousins would stand up, turn to face the seated fans and then we would bow several times and throw kisses with our hands to our audience. We did this each Saturday, so much so, the audience would call us to stand up and bow.

What a delightful time we had. Each of us looked forward to being at our grandparents each summer.

I remember our childhood Christmases at grand moms. Again everyone went home upstate to grand moms. On her fireplace hung a stocking for each child. I can still see my aunts stringing popcorn for the Christmas Tree. Those were spectacular days, memories that are imbedded in our hearts. We were blessed with our family in Shamokin, they taught us how to be a family filled with love and respect. Ralph loved the attention of everyone because they fussed over him and embellished him with hugs and kisses...lots of love. Our grandfather would give us each a dollar bill. We would line up, walk to him while saying Merry Christmas grandpa and he would had each of us the dollar. That was a big deal. In the 50's it was really a giant-ic deal.

Ralphs father passed away at seventy from a heart attack. Ralph would not come home for his funeral. A month or so later Ralph appeared out of nowhere and mom cried from happiness seeing him. She begged him to stay home with her, that the two of them could be happy and live in peace. Ralph stayed home a few weeks but he missed the ranch that one night he just simply left without notice. Poor mom, she was so beside herself. Would she ever be able to depend on Ralph's company.

My daughter was in 7th grade and spent weeks at my mothers during the summer. Karan loved being with her and she had many friends in mom's neighborhood. I picked up Karan to take her home and get her school supplies. Mom began to cry and begged me to let Karan go to school and live with her. I dreaded this moment and knew it was coming. My mom knew that I had a hard time saying no to her but I firmly said NO,...

Mom was invited to move in my home. She knew all of my neighbors and often said how niece it was in my neighborhood. I really wanted her to move in with me and my family. I offered to take care of her but she desperately pleaded with me to let Karan stay with her. NO, again NO. Mom stated that she couldn't because she had to keep the house for when Ralph would come home......NO

Mom would stay with us on weekends and longer times when she was released from the hospital. To recuperate. She enjoyed her stays because she wasn't alone and she was close to Karan and my son Rob. They loved her so much. They felt her gentleness and love. No matter how sick she was, they were blessed with her hugs and kisses. I always hated to see mom go home and be alone in her house.

I worried about her safety along with the fact she is alone. And then, mom passed away.

Moms sick ridden body finally gave way. It was strange how I felt that day. Something was wrong with her, I thought. I had talked to her several times that week but this one day, I couldn't get in touch with her. I called every girlfriend of hers and tried several times to trace her normal routine.

Something is gravely wrong with her. More calls and I still couldn't get in touch with her. Everyone she often visited. No one saw her in the last twenty four hours. I began to panic. I called her Neighbor, Millie and asked her to check her house. Millie was terribly upset when she called me after checking moms house. I instantly interrupted her and screamed my moms dead isn't she. Poor Millie.

The police were called and the city hospital. They told me she died while sleeping on her couch. The coroner said she was dead two days. That news tripled my hurt for her loss.

We couldn't reach Ralph by phone so we had an Alert put out on him through police at the county he lived. The police found him and informed him about mom, she was deceased. Ralph came home the next day. The ranch owner had one of his hands drive Ralph to the door. Moms body was placed at a friends parlor. My cousins helped with arrangements and which cemetery to place her. I chose the one nearest my residence. I wanted her close.

Our family upstate made the trip for moms funeral. Three aunts, Rita, Beatrice and Gloria immediately came to help me with moms house. They did each room. First get rid of what wasn't needed. Cousin Ken contacted a household buyer to take anything that wouldn't be used or needed.

I gave Ken and his family all the food in storage shelves and refrigerator, and whatever items he and his wife needed. Ken also sold moms refrigerator, I told Ken to keep the money he got from the sell. My aunts and I then began to clean the house from top to bottom. We then gathered all of moms clothes my aunt Beatrice took them to give to certain neighbors she knew that could use them. The next chore was to close the house. Years of taxes were owed on the property so we had to let the city have it.

Moms death took it's toll on me. I began my day crying and went to her grave site every day after work and again I would cry uncontrollably. This emotional train lasted for sic months. I felt I lost my mind and couldn't' sleep. I took prescriptions to help me survive. I was an absolute mess. Thank God, my employer was compassionate and kept me on. I looked like hell. My job saved me from total collapse.

Ralph stayed on and lived with us. My husband got him a job with the city's water department as a sweeper. He lived with us about a year but couldn't stand the city any longer and went back to the ranch to live. He said he needed to be there to fill peace and love with the Animals. Ralph would say People hurt you, animals don't'.

I kept in touch with Ralph and kept close watch on his money. Occasionally he would request a few hundred so that he could purchase a horse. Ralph would buy a horse, groom it, feed it and sell the horse at a small profit. Some of their horses looked like old nags ready to die. Ralph would redeem the horse to a point that a buyer would pay his price. Ralph knew and loved animals and it offended him that some horse owners would neglect them to a stage where they weren't well. This was where his love of animals and the attention he gave them paid off. He devoted his love and care to the animals.

Ralph had two pure white peacocks named Romeo and Juliet. How he loved those birds and took many pictures of them to show to everyone.

Later those peacocks gave him eight babies and each one was pure white. White peacocks are valuable and offers to buy them were always an issue. Ralph would not part with his 'love couple.'

Ralphs health began to decline. Remember I stated that after Ralphs birth, he came home from the hospital with glass casts on his legs. He began to have a difficult time walking and the owners of the ranch called me to suggested Ralph come home to live with me so that I can take care of him. They explained that if he can't work for his room and board, he couldn't live there. I asked them to have one of their workers drive him home and I will pay that person $100.00 dollars. The very next day Ralph was delivered to me. I was in shock seeing how bad Ralphs condition was. I could see the pain in his face that he was feeling.

I sat Ralph in the kitchen and quietly tried to find the source of his pain so that I knew what to tell the doctor for his visit the next day. I asked Ralph to tell me every spot on his body that was hurting. He calmly told me that it was his feet.

I then knelt down and unlaced his boots so that I could take them off. I couldn't believe what I found. Ralph's boots were attached to his skin. Oh my God, my poor brother. Please God help me help my brother by not causing him more pain. Guide me as I touch his feet.

I filled a basin with warm water and poured witch hazel in it. I didn't know what else to use.

I began the delicate job of removing the leather of his boot from his skin. I did this slowly and carefully so as not to cause him more added pain. I kept asking Ralph if he was he okay. I laid his foot on a clean towel. proceeded to take the first boot off. I cleaned his foot with a medicated rinse and laid his foot on a medicated towel. I then did the same treatment to his second foot. Both feet were boot free clean and medicated. I then made sure Ralph had a good supper and told him that I prepared a room for him. He was exhausted and wanted to sleep. I was restless and was filled with anguish after seeing Ralph's condition. I couldn't sleep. I sat in the TV room remembering Ralph' childhood and his pre and teen years. He had a hard life finding a way to take care of himself. The abuse he took and the lonely years of being treated as if he didn't matter. My heart could explode with the sadness he suffered. His disabilities made him a charmer and a clown. He loved making you laugh. Ralph sensed our mothers discomfort and make effort to bring a smile on her face.

Ralphs favorite times were at the stables with the horses. He loved caring for them. His goal in life was to be a rancher. Who was to know that through running away from home would make his dream a reality. This was only part of his dream, he also wanted to travel to different states that he hadn't seen and the rest of Canada. He got to Canada when he joined their traveling circus. Seeing other states and parts of Canada, he felt made those years worthwhile.

Several years ago he made connections with a wonderful family, who appreciated him and offered him a position with them at their ranch. They were true to their word, Ralph was with them almost 20 years. This ranch was also a training place where people came to learn how to ride horses. They made the importance of giving good care to the horse and the running of a clean stable environment.

Once Ralphs chores were complete he was able to do whatever he wanted. He often went fishing, which was another love of his life. He purchased a small boat from a flea market so he could float in the nearby lake, cast his line and simply enjoy his day. Ralph loved the peace of the outdoors. He often said that nothing compared to what his freedom gave him. He was a simple man and wanted nothing more in life but to exist in peace. I feel blessed having Ralph as my bother. He taught me forgiveness, patience and a love that cannot be explained. A love of ones sibling that cannot be compared. He filled my life with joy and for that lam grateful to have experienced knowing him and being part of his life.

Forgiveness was hard for me concerning Ralph. I felt he was cheated in life by not having the chance I had living with my grandparents. I had to forgive his father. Ralph did make excuses for him, instead he would say that his dad couldn't do more considering the hard times he had with high medical bills and the lack of work. I never realized that Ralph saw things so clearly as he did. He was smarter and more clever than anyone thought him to be.

Back to Ralph and plans to get his health back:

The next day Ralph met my doctor. I had spoken to the doctor re: Ralphs condition. Ranch hands aren't the cleanest people. They live with animals and smell like them to. No insult intended, just a truthful comment. I always felt that my doctor was sincere in caring for his patients but after I witnessed the Doctor take care of Ralph, I believed he was saintly. He examined Ralph with gentleness, compassion and thought-fullness. He knelt on his knees while talking to him. Looking right into Ralphs eyes as he spoke gently and caring,. He explaining everything that he believed was a health issue for Ralph and made sure Ralph understood the seriousness of what must be done to insure Ralph gets well again. My, no our doctor in fact made all the appointments for the specialists to see Ralph. He had the doctors co-operation in lining up appointments in succession so that with a few weeks, not months, Ralph would be seen and taken care of.

The first doctor Ralph saw was a foot specialist. He diagnosed that Ralph had a rare foot fungus. It was serious and needed immediate attention. I had to bathe his feet every night then apply the medication. As his feet healed I had to file all dead skin on his feet and apply the new medication on the new skin., took two months of constant care and it worked. Ralph could then walk without pain. I of course threw away his old boots and purchased good foamy slippers for him to get around.

Now the Orthopedic specialist. Prior to the visit I had taken Ralph for all the x rays needed. The doctor explained what was found. Ralph's hip joints would eventually have to be replaced. Ralph's condition the doctor said began at birth.

His hips were abnormally formed. This caused Ralph to walk with an unusual gait. The doctor estimated the operation would be needed between 2 to 4 years. The doctor gave us instructions and Ralph blurted out, "my sister will take care of everything for me". I felt a flow of peace flow thru me when he said that. To me it meant he trusted me and knew I would take care of him.

Ralph was so gentle, kind and never complained. I'd come home from work and he would give me time to get changed into my comfort clothes and then tease me by saying, 'come on sis, rattle those pots and pans'. Meaning lets get dinner started. I would say back to him that I spoiled him and he would reply, 'you should I'm the baby brother'.

Every morning before I went to work, I prepared his breakfast and lunch. All he had to do was heat the meals in the microwave. I put on a fresh coffee pot, and make fresh ice tea, and load the frig with other drinks. He was set for the day.

One evening I noticed at dinner that Ralph was staring in to space. Immediately I realized he was having a seizure. It didn't last long and Ralph didn't he realize he just had a seizure. This brought back memories when he was a baby and would seizure several times a day. Thank God the episodes didn't occur frequently and did not alter Ralph's temperament. They frightened me as a child.

I could see the improvement in Ralph's health each day. I really enjoyed him being here with us. Every two weeks I would get the clippers and cut Ralph's hair. He really didn't like care for the short hair and warned me that when he was well and his self again, he was growing his hair long, really long. I just laughed.

During Ralph's first month living with us, he was taken to 20 doctor appointments, which included several specialists that required initial and returns visits. Our primary doctor saw him every week until he felt Ralph was well enough health wise and made his return visits on a monthly basis. Some of the test he had to under go caused him discomfort but he never complained or gave me a hard time. He liked all of the doctors and they were pleased to see how well he recovered. I was relieved to see Ralph feeling so good and able to get around without aide.

After dinner Ralph and I cleaned up the kitchen and we'd go outside and sit on the patio with our neighbors. We would socialize until 8 or 8:30 and go back into the house and watch TV shows. I would go to bed around 10 pm because of work the next day. Ralph would be up all hours and that was okay. He could sleep as late as he wanted to... and that was also okay.

The big day was coming for Ralph. His special shoes were ready to be picked. The podiatrist, who helped save Ralph's feet wrote a prescription for shoes that would help improve his gait and more importantly would be much more comfortable. He told Ralph that he must continue with the treatments that I gave him every night on his feet, especially wearing the new boot-shoes. I made it a point to massage and treat his feet every night after dinner.

How exciting it was to see Ralph walk around like any normal person. He stood 6'2" and his gait was great. Ralph would take long walks while I was working. His cousin Ken was laid off and they would take long trips to the ranch and everyone there couldn't believe how good Ralph looked and how now he could get around so well. Ralph and cousin Ken would take off once a week.

Horse shows, flea markets and auctions filled their day. They both enjoyed their time together and would come home laughing and talking about their day. I was so happy to see Ralph happiness and smiles.

Winter is on its way and my thoughts were about how Ralph would do in the city. I was afraid of boredom and loneliness for him. People didn't hang out on their patios in the winter, so there wouldn't be the socializing he had gotten used to. He didn't have his cousin Ken or Jim to run around with. Both had found jobs again and had to work to support their families.

It only took a few weeks into the fall months and Ralph asked if could go back to the ranch to live. I painfully had to tell him that he could never go back to live. The owners of the ranch had the ranch up for sale with hopes to live a better life without the burden of the ranch. They didn't want the responsibility of another persons life. And they just wanted a simpler way of living.

Ralph's heart was broken and felt trapped living with me. He had nothing to do and missed the ranch very much. It kept him busy. Ralph stated that he was a grown man and wanted a place of his own. He said that he really appreciated everything I did for him and promised to take better of himself, just like I taught him. It touched me deeply when Ralph said that I was like the mother he missed having when growing up and that he loved me.

Ralph was serious about living on his own. His happiness was more important to me than having him live here. The protectiveness I felt for Ralph had to be put aside. The realization that yes, he is a grown man and is now able to live on his own. I have taught him a lot while he has been here with me. He learned well how to care of himself. A new life lesson he was never taught, until now, from me. Ralph has learned well and I will find him a good place to live.

I began looking into apartments nearby for Ralph but everything was so expensive, not affordable on his income. I called my cousin Jack from Shamokin, Pa. Jack was self employed in construction and owned several apartments. I asked Jack to help me find a place for Ralph. I wanted to purchase a duplex building. Ralph could live on the first floor and we could rent the second floor to help pay the mortgage. I was willing to go into debt for Ralph because I loved him and wanted his happiness and independence. Ralph liked the idea living up state. He could have other family and be in a small town where he could walk to where ever he was planning to go.

My cousin Jack found three properties for Ralph and I to see. It was only a three hour drive and we could stay at my cousins overnight. We planned to do this over the weekend but later my cousin, Jack called me back and said he thought things over and decided that I was crazy to take on another mortgage at my age. He offered to call a few favors in town and get my brother into a county run apartment building where the rent went according to income and you must be 50 and over. He said the building was beautiful and well maintained and spotless. It sounded so good to be true. Ralph and I said yes and would be there during the weekend.

Good new! There were three apartments to choose from. Ralph chose an efficiency on the third floor. I put down the security deposited and first months rent, and they gave Ralph the key to his new residence. Ralph beamed with excitement.

Now to furnish it while we were there. Jack took us to a second hand shop. They had a nice selection and we purchased a living room and kitchen set and a large dresser for his clothes. Jack had a twin bed and gave that to Ralph. His apartment is now furnished. The apartment had two large closets and a smaller storage closet. Ralph was so excited and happy of the location from town...only three blocks.

Now to go back to Philly to shop for essentials like dishes, pot and pans, towels for kitchen and bath and a shower curtain with hooks, silverware and dishes, glassware, and all other odds and ends that are needed. Food and spices and other refrigerate items will be picked up once we are back in Shamokin.

Back in Philly I made a list of everything to be purchased. I looked in my cupboards as I made the lists so that nothing will be forgotten. My granddaughters and I went shopping and bought all items on my list. We even purchased decorations for Ralphs apartment. Now the trick was to pack carefully and fit everything into my mid sized car and trunk. We made the trip during the weekend. We spilt the work, my granddaughter, Candace was in charge of setting up the kitchen while I was to buy all of the food from the list I made. I made sure that Ralph was stocked on meals, snacks, etc.

I also purchased a small micro-wave, shades for his two windows, curtains will be on my next trip.

I also put in an order for his telephone and TV cable connection. Ralph looked around his apartment and he filled up with tears. A few of our relatives lived one block up the street and that was our aunt Judy and uncle Jim. They would walk their dog down the street and look up to Ralphs window on the third floor and say hello. And they did this every morning and screamed up to him saying "Ralph, I love you" and Ralph would scream back "I love you too", They waved together and Ralph felt love and burst with happiness.

I explained where everything was and where our grandparents used to live. Their store was still there connected to their house. The store was still opened and my uncle GiB ran it. The uncles and cousins used to get together each morning at the store for coffee and to chat.

I told Ralph how easy it was to find the store/ house. This would be a healthy walk for him and a time to get to know his extended family. I pre-told everyone by email that I was bringing Ralph to live there. It was time to leave Ralph and head back to Philly. Ralph and I both began to fill up with tears. I told Ralph how much I will miss him and how much I loved him. Again Ralph told me he loved me and will miss me. I reassured him that I would come up twice a month to clean for him. Ralph reminded me to post a note on the community room boaard for a cleaning person. l posted a note and put Ralphs phone number on the board. He knew what to say, I had it written down. I also left a personal phone book by his phone with all phone numbers and addresses of our family of those who lived upstate.

Well its time for me to head back to Philly. We promised to call on the weekend that I wasn't making the trip. We had time together when I was most needed by Ralph. Now its his time to be grown up and take care of himself.

Two weeks went by and Hooray we hired a cleaning woman. She would work twice a month and go through his efficiency apartment. And more great news, Jack got Ralph a primary Doctor. All his medical records were sent to him so that he could care for Ralph.

Ralph found auctions to go to and other days he would walk through town and window shop. He often stopped at our family coffee clutch where the family gathered every morning. He made several friends at his building and they would gather at the local coffee shop in town.

Ralph loved living upstate. He would call me just to tell me how happy he was. I would fill up with tears of joy and thankfulness. Ralph was so gentle and kind. It was about time he had happiness and love in his life. Living upstate where most of our family lived, opened invitations for Ralph on holidays and family picnics. He enjoyed being included in all family functions. He felt loved.

It was so wonderful of the ranch people, who Ralph worked for call him every month and sometimes send him a big box of his favorite candies and treats. Ralph would always ask about his white peacocks, Romeo and Juliet. He left them with the ranch owners to keep. They loved Ralph and would fill him in on all the news at the ranch. They did love him and they miss him. Christmas was on its way and shopping was a serious business. Ralph gave me a list on the phone and I promised to surprise him.

The kids were coming home and Ralph was looking forward being with all of us for the holidays. I sent him bus money and purchased a large suitcase for him to take his presents to his home upstate. Decorations and a lot of cooking and baking went on during weekends to be prepared to have plenty for everyone. I wrapped presents as I purchased them so that I didn't have that headache at the last minute. Everyone was excited about the holidays and seeing one another and we all planned to make this holiday special for Ralph.

It was a joyful time for everyone. We love being together and this was more meaningful because Ralph is with us. Everyone got Ralph gifts. As I gave him our gifts, I saw tears in his eyes and they melted my heart. He said he never expected so much and we explained that we wanted to spoil him because we have him back in our lives.

The holidays were over and everyone went home. Ralph went back upstate with his large suite case and I began to take down the decorations Wow! Such a great holiday. All the love to keep us warm during the winters months.

Winter that year was cold and snowy. I wasn't able to travel upstate more than once a month to see Ralph. We kept in contact each week by phone. He would call me and as I would pick up the he would sing "1 just called to say I love you". I'd fill up with tears and cry from happiness.

I would ask Ralph each time we talked if he was really happy living upstate and he would answer that he didn't like it.....HE LOVED IT. You cannot imagine how relieved and grateful to God I was. Everyone loved Ralph. They saw how gentle, generous and loving he was. Mom was noted for her gentleness, and loving nature too.

I did manage to visit Ralph three or four times during the winter months. Each time while there

I would disinfect and scrub everything spotless. Sometimes I would order dinner for us. That night I would get my pillow and blanket from the closet and sleep in the floor. I enjoyed doing things for Ralph. I felt good inside. I was paying an owed debt because always felt Ralph got zero end of breaks in life. I was fortunate because I was rescued by my grandparents. He wasn't.

How things change in a few years. Ralph was doing so well health wise for the first three years living on his own upstate. Remember what the orthopedic doctor warned...Ralph would eventually need hip replacement, most likely within a two to four year period. Time passes by so quickly and Ralph was now going into his fourth year being independent and enjoying his life.

His hips finally gave out. His gait worsened each month, week, day. He painfully struggled to get by. I called my cousin Bill to take Ralph to his doctor appointments and to find a good Orthopedic doctor to look into Ralph's hip condition. Bill wasted no time getting Ralph a new primary and specialist.

Appointments were set, test were ordered and suggested treatments were to be followed before considering surgery of any kind. This went on for a few months and Ralph's condition only worsened. In fact cousin Bill ordered a wheelchair from Medicare for Ralph to use. The chair helped Ralph get around more comfortably. He had a lot of pain and the surgery became a wish for the surgery to happen was the only thing Ralph looked forward to.

I was scheduled for a total hysterectomy, on April 26. I received a call from Ralph that his surgery was scheduled for the 27th. They were only doing one hip at a time and would schedule the second hip surgery six months later. I couldn't cancel surgery because I had a condition that had to be taken care of immediately. I was also in pain and already put in for the time off work. I explained this to Ralph and we both decided I would be upstate to help him after was released from rehabilitation which would take me into two weeks recouping from my surgery. I would stay with Ralph in his apartment and care of him. I would take the rest of my vacation time off to be with him. We take walks, visit relatives and just loaf together.

My surgery cane and all went well. Ralph called me later the day after his surgery and told me that they had him walking around the hospital. He said it wasn't to bad because he was on a morphine drip. Ralph was so excited about being able to move his new hip and not have pain in his leg and groin and he couldn't wait to get the other hip replaced. Ralph wanted the other hip replaced sooner because he wanted to travel.

In Canada and upstate New York, Ralph had friends that invited him to visit and tour their area. We talked about his new freedom and how wonderful for Ralph be able to plan his life. He was grateful that he will no longer be obligated or obligated and feel he imposes on another person. After all Ralph cared about people and did not want to oppose on their lives.

Our last conversation was four days after both of our surgeries. Ralph did his daily walk in the hospital and as usual he would sit in his chair and watch the traffic at the nurses station. A nurse would wake him to take his medication and the day would proceed. Medication time, Ralph, wake up...But Ralph didn't wake up. He passed on.

I never got to say goodbye. He had several visitors that day and got tired so he did his thing, sit by the nurse station and fall asleep. That was around l:pm. My cousin Bill called me around 12:30 PM and by his choking, gasping words, I got the news I never expected, Ralph died in his sleep. Both Bill and I cried hysterically.

Month prior to Ralph's death, I went with my cousin Dennis to the funeral parlor a few blocks from Ralphs apartment. I made arrangements for Ralph to be cremated and to have a room to invite family and friends to his memorial services. I was also able to purchased a plot at the cemetery where my grandparents and other family were buried. I also hired a room and caterer for after the funeral services where everyone could meet and have dinner. Almost 40 people paid homage to my brother.

My daughter and I spent hours preparing picture collages of Ralph with differently family member and the functions he attended from their invite. I never expected myself to outlive my brother. He was so relaxed and I was always stressed. Oh my God, my heart hurts with such pain in loosing him. My sweet, gentle brother. His innocence and truthfulness was so like our moms.

THE BANANA TABLE

As I look back my memory tells me... we tried desperately to prove them Wong. They woe all in agreement that we would not make it. In fact, bets were made as to how long we would stay together. We both came from low income, and somewhat dysfunctional families. Both families woe struggling to keep their heads above water What little help they could provide would not be offered immediately. They wanted to see how we would provide for ourselves. We didn't expect them to bail us out if the need came. We knew it wasn't right to count on anyone, after all, this is what we chose to do. Together we swore we would prove them wrong. Our determination was to work haul and make a decent life for us and any children we would have. We didn't realize then that coming from a small town would make our goals a lot harder to attain.

We started with $57.00 in our bank account, found an apartment and second hand furniture. To us this was paradise. We both worked in the county's shoe factory. Not the best jobs but we were earning week/v checks to pay our way and save for our future. We were independent, proud and hopeful for the tomorrows that laid ahead That is until the layoff's occurred. I was let go first. As upsetting as it was, we could still get by on his paycheck. And so it was. We managed fine for a few months, but then came the news of expecting our first child. A most precious moment of great news clouded by the dismissal of my husbands department. He too was let go. What to do, what to do.

News of this reached our families and to our surprise help was offered. A part time job for my husband At my uncles store as delivery man starting immediately. This was a great help to us and we managed by being tight with the dollar. No spending at all, no entertainment. We didn't go out except to visit filmily. Family on both sides would invite us for dinners, this in itself allowed a huge savings on food. Our friends would come to our place and always brought beverages and would Older pizza. We had friends that would go to any length to give a hand and had promises of babysitting so we could have a night out. So things were still great. We felt lucky and still looked forward to making our lives more secure and successful.

———

Job hunting was a most depressing episode for my husband. He finally landed a job at a supermarket but only part time, so he continued to do deliveries for my uncle. With both pays, we managed just fine. And then came the baby. I went into labor five weeks early. The delivery was natural, the time was too many hours of haul labor and many stitches. A daughter was born. She was so tiny. Five and a half pounds. When I held her, I would gaze at this little angel in amazement and thank God for her safe delivery. Everyone came to see her The doctors and nurses loved when my grandmother would visit, for she always came with baskets of fresh fruit for them and the two women sharing my mom.

Everyone in the county knew my grandparents. They had the closest family in the city. A whopping eighteen children and never on welfare. My grandparents welt? very prideful, hard work was the way to become self-efficient was their belief.' Their beginning in this country was haul. My grandfather pushed a cart filled with fresh vegetables and went from neighborhood to neighborhood selling his produce. Years later, his oldest sons did the same while my grandfather sold his goods in a horse and buggy. And later he opened his first stow. Soon after he had t/llee Italian Supermarkets in town. Their seven daughters married and had families of their own. Ten sons, each of-whom served our country in different wars from WWII, Korean, and Viet Nam. The youngest son died in a plane crash over swamps, his body was never recovered. My grandmother cried every morning over the loss of her son, then got herself together and went on to cook and care for her family.

What deep gratitude I have for my grandparents. I lived with them all through high school. They have instilled in me the love and importance of family and good work ethics. It was always wonderful to visit them and get all the hugs and kisses I missed since graduating Dom high school. While living with my grandparents, I learned how to prepare and jar vegetables and tomatoes and even preserves by aiding my grandmother and aunts. Every late August and early September preparing these foods for winter was the most important chore. I have great memories and good times while living with my grandparents. I can only hope that all I have learned from them leads me to live a life such as theirs.

It wasn't long, I'd say five months after our daughter was born when we realized that we had to move to a city in order to find decent employment. We were going into a hole of debt trying to survive. My family lived in Philadelphia and invited us to move in with them until we got jobs and could go on our own. My mother couldn't wait to have our daughter all to herself. And so made the move to the big city.

All our personal belongings were packed in banana boxes. We would have to start over

Our furniture was passed among friends who since got married and was happy to take certain pieces. It was haul moving from our small town and the friends we were close to. The total environment of living in a small town was peaceful and welcoming. A great place to raise a family. Yet we had to leave so that we could better provide for ourselves and our daughter And so we came to the big city to live where the prospects of decent jobs were offered. All of our hopes were in banana boxes from my uncles store.

My husband was the first to land a job. Though my aunt, who lived in Philadelphia, and her connections, he was hired at a long standing plant making wood stains. I didn't get work the first few months because I spent my time cleaning and painting my mom's home. She had health problems and couldn't do strenuous chores, therefore there was much to be done. All went well because my stepfather was pleased to see his home in order and he enjoyed the baby. So it seemed things were working out.

Now time to find myself a job. I took employment as a part time waitress so that my mother wasn't babysitting full time. It would be too hard on her Even though she loved having the baby, I knew her poor health wouldn't allow her to watch her fill time. All the lifting to change diapers, etc, would not be good for mom. This arrangement seemed to work out good My mother's neighborhood in South Philly was great. All the neighbors were very close to one another I grew up in that block and had friends who were still at home and we continued on with our friendship. It was comfortable and I felt safe and happy.

My husband made friends with the fellas I grew up with. They got a kick out of him because of his ignorance Q/the city. They made him feel like one of the boys and they invited him to share in their interest, one of which was drag car racing. Wow, you couldn't have offered my husband a better thing to do. Up state the big entertainment for the guys was drag racing in the mountains. The Philly guys introduced my husband to a fella that owned a gas station where they rebuilt cars to race, and of course did car repairs and sold gas. This was paradise to my husband and he made a deal with the owner to let him help work on cars and go to the races with him and he would give him ten hours a week helping at his station, after his work hours.

Drag racing was big in our neighborhood. You either went to the well known drag strips and competed or some evenings you would join in with the illegal drag racing behind the large warehouses near the navy yard. There would be dozens of us there watching or racing. The police most of the time ignored us being there as long as everyone behaved themselves. In fact there were a few policemen with hot cars who raced with the gang. I was in a policeman's race car an old 32 roadster when some on duty police came to clear us out because of complaints. Our crowds became to large and surrounding communities demanded us to leave the premises. Almost 200 persons were arrested that night and the news hit all the local newspapers. I wasn't one of them because of being with the officer. No one was kept and no charges were made. It was just a loud message that a crowd that huge will not be allowed to gather there without a permit. These woe many fun times. We made new friends and met them at least one night a week to watch racing and eat pizza.

In South Philly, once your accepted, your a friend for life. The neighborhood we lived in was a conglomerate of Jewish, Irish, Italian and Polish nationalities. The women kept our block so clean. They daily washed the white marble steps and swept any dirt found on the street and sidewalks. Most surrounding city blocks were the same. People took pride in their neighborhood. No one was rich but everyone was prideful with their property. Giving up we were taught respect of our elders and chores were apart of life. Today, it shamefully isn't that way. Certain areas have declined to the point of becoming a slum area because of neglect and laziness. There are those who think it is owed to them to have everything handed to them.

We made a trip upstate at least once a month. We'd stay with relatives and visited our many friends. It was always good to go home and see everyone. Most of our friends were now expecting their first child. All of our lives were changing and soon, one by one a friend would have to move to find work. Our small town was sliding backwards. Stores were closing, movies shut down and the lace malls outside the town were not hiring full time or needing as many employees. All anyone could find was part time work. The economy was in a rut and forcing people to look elsewhere to live and work in order to survive. Our pretty little town was becoming a boarded up nightmare. Progress is great as long as the 'big shots' remember the middle class. Problem is they don't. Their profits are mow important than the people who work hard for them. What is to become of the middle class? People say that eventually, there won't be but rich and poor in our country. How sad and discouraging for those who are stuck there and can't move on or simply have no other alternative.

And so, we both had our jobs, lived with my mom and stepfather. In time we paid off our debts from our home town and began to save so we could move into our own place. Summer was coming and our daughter would be one year old. My mother insisted we get an Italian Creme Cake. We set up a table outside and invited the neighbors to have cake. A simple celebration with people we were happy to be around. The neighbors called my daughter 'Pebbles' like the cartoon girl in the 'Flintstones' because I often combed her hair up to keep it out of her eyes. She looked really adorable.

Later in the year, we found housing in a City Project. Very affordable rent that included all utilities. It at the time was a beautiful project and well cared for by the city. The yards and gardens were pruned and mowed weekly and the streets woe kept very clean. I liked living there because it really gave us a chance to get ahead. Shortly after moving there, I found an office job that paid benefits and a decent wage. It was close to the project so I walked to attend work every day.

When we moved into the project we had no furniture other than our newly purchased bedrooms. We bought them while living with my parents before we moved. We had nothing to sit down and have dinner on and couldn't buy anything else until our bed moms were paid in full. That was our rule. One room at a time and no mounting debts. I was clever on creating a dinette set with two banana boxes put together with packing tape, two brass trash cans as chairs, a nice table cloth and candles. WA La, we had a place to have our meals. Our daughter had her little kitchen set next to us with her dolls as her guest and we had our meals there until I was able to purchase a real dinette set. As fun as it was, the 'Banana Table' I called it, gave me the initiative to save, save, save.

My job went well and I met wonderful girls, who I became friendly and close with. I enjoyed work.

Within a few months I was offered a promotion to 'Keypunch Operator'. They trained me and I was given a nice raise. I loved learning and went on to be a Keypunch Auditor and received another raise. We banked every dime we could so that we could buy furniture, one room at a time. The project learned of my promotions and salary and we notified that we had to move. They impressed upon us that we had a chance to get ahead, now it was time to give another couple that same advantage. How could we not feel that we should move. We were very grateful that we were able to have that bleak. And so, we looked for an apartment.

Hooray! A two bed mom apartment was in the paper in an area we knew was good. We went to see it, loved it, and we applied for it. Good news, we got it. We were to move in two weeks. Apart from banana boxes with our clothes, kitchen ware, our bed mom sets, it didn't take much to move out. Friends helped us and we were in and settled in one day. The apartment was further from work for me and taking a bus would mean getting up an hour earlier each day. I did this for a few weeks and finally made a connection with a women, who had a carpool. She agreed to pick me up and bring me home each day. On the way to work, I was her last pickup. On the way home, I was her first off. This made going to work a lot less stressful. After a few weeks we were able to buy a dinette set. Hooray! No mow banana boxes as our table and trash cans as our seats.

I would visit my mom on weekends or she would come to our apartment. It was a bus and trolley ride and took almost an hour to and from. I wasn't annoyed with the ride because I would set my mind to enjoy the quiet time and look at the scenery. I kept on thinking how grateful I was for the good in my life. I couldn't believe how far we have come in the past two years. One day, while on a trolley car, I saw the living room set of my dreams. I saw this same set in a magazine and dream t of owning it. I pulled the pulley to let the driver know to stop, got off the trolley and went into the store to purchase the furniture. I was so happy and anxious to get home to tell my husband. We didn't have furniture in the living room because we were saving for it. Remember; one room at a time. We had to wait almost six months for the furniture because the store I purchased it from only sold ten of the same set in the entire city. They sold only original sets and they weren't made until all ten sets were sold. The wait was worth it. I loved my living mom. It was elegant and classy.

Color TV was popular and we had a black and white set. Well, finances were decent so I purchased our first color TV It was a beautiful piece of furniture, cherry wood finish that matched the wood on our living room set. How exciting for us to have such a lovely room in our apartment. 0111 kitchen and two bedrooms were pretty but our living room was beautiful. Too prideful you think...no and yes. We were proud of our accomplishments but we were also grateful for what we had and worked so hard for. We had good friends and decent jobs, a beautiful and healthy daughter; what more could you ask for.

This isn't Utopia. Life is filled with ups and downs. My husband fell in work and his injuries caused almost six months of unemployment. Back then you didn't have workmen's comp and you couldn't collect unemployment if you could not work. So it was my pay to live on which was manageable except for the Icoge hospital bill and doctors fees. My mother would bring us meats for weeks at a time and this was of the greatest help. She shared whatever she could afford. I was able to spread our grocery money further because of her generosity. And life goes on and you learn discipline in all aspects during these trials.

Back on our feet, we are both working again and are concentrating getting out of the medical debts. We have all we need material wise, thereof, we should be able to zero out all owed monies. Life is good again, now it's time to breathe easier and enjoy living. Thanksgiving was here and I was preparing a huge turkey for us and my family. I was so looking forward to this holiday and having my parents stay overnight. But bliss doesn't last forever My husband took ill. He was doubled up in pain and we had to call an ambulance to take him to the hospitals ER. Surprisingly within a half hour a doctor came to talk with me to explain my husband had appendicitis and was being taken to the operating room immediately. His appendix burst and infection already set in. After one week he was released but it was to soon, for he ran a high fever in the hospital and should never have been released. While at home he seemed to get worse with pain and continued to run a high fever. He was admitted again into the hospital and was operated on that same day. The new attending physician said he was filled with infection and they had to put tubing in him so the infection would drain out. This doctor agreed with me that the first surgeon should not have released him with a fever...this meant the infection was not cleared up. He could have died.

Six weeks of care at home and seeing the new stuᵣgeon on a weekly basis, finally my husband was back to being healthy. This experience was horrible for the both of us. I used vacation days to take care of him for the first two weeks but had to go back to work. I was confident he was strong enough to be by himself I left his lunch prepared for him and I called him on my lunch break. We managed on just my salary but once again we were faced with doctor and hospital bills piled up. Life must go on so you pick yourself up and get into a new frame of mind to start over.

Christmas was here and it was a lean one as far as gifts went. My mother and stepfather came to stay overnight for the holiday and Christmas dinner We had snow, just enough to cover the ground and this made the atmosphere feel more playful for our daughter She was expecting Santa and knew he was coming on his sleigh with reindeer to deliver gifts to all good children and Santa needed snow. The holiday went well and dinner was better than I expected for I made my first goose.

It seemed we were cursed with health issues for my husband. The seven years we were in the apartment, he was in the hospital once each year.

Mostly for kidney problems. Thank God that he didn't need surgeries but this sure put a damper on our finances. Again when you face these issues, you can't give up. As hard and depressing as those times were, we didn't give up. It was starting over again and again. It was either that or sink and go back to the projects and neither of us wanted that.

Surprise, I'm pregnant again and this time the pregnancy is good. I had a few miscarriages and was told that I would not be able to have another child. Our daughter was now five and a half and when we told her that she might have a brother or sister, she was so happy and couldn't wait until the baby was born. He was absolutely beautiful. Pitch black hail; dark eyes and the cutest little chubby boy. My bundle of joy.

I was about eight months pregnant when my husband went into the hospital again. He doubled up in pain and had to be taken by ambulance. My neighbor took me to the hospital and his wife took care of our daughter while I was gone. Thank God, this time it wasn't a long stay. It turned out to be a strain in his groin a fall at work. He was home within two days, and life went on. I had a boy and named him after his daddy. Our daughter loved him. I would let her help me with little things so that she was a part of his care. I could see their bond instantly. Our son was absolutely beautiful. A full head of pitch black hail,' dark brown eyes and a little chubby bundle of joy.

As I said, we lived in the apartment for seven years. As good tenants, we paid our rent on time and kept our apartment and joining steps clean. In fact our landlord praised us constantly for being such responsible and caring people. One day we were informed by his sister; who lived downstairs that we had to move. She was upset about it because we became such good friends. Out landlord was her brother and their mother wasn't able to live alone anymore so they wanted the apartment for her It would be so good for her to be with family but in her own apartment with her daughter downstairs to look in on her etc. They welt' good people and we blended as family for those seven years.

What to do, what to do. We thought about what we wanted and decided it was time to buy a house. And so the hunt began. House hunting can be very stressful, especially when you are limited in what you can spend. I did the most searching by real estates and the newspaper. We went to look at a few houses but for the asking price and the location or condition the house was in, put such a damper on hope of finding a decent property. I wanted our house to be in a good neighborhood and would not settle for less.

My cousin lived about five miles from where our apartment was and she called me to tell me that a friend of hers told her about a new development she moved into. This was only three blocks from my cousins house. The price range was what we could afford so we arranged to go and see the houses with hope that our bid would be accepted. We chose one of the smaller homes because of price. It was a laid out nicely and I imagined immediately where all of our furniture would go.

The bid was denied. We were devastated but placed another bid and it was accepted. We would make settlement and move within six weeks. The challenge now was how to get the entire down payment and settlement cost together We had saving bonds deducted from my husband's pay and ignored them for several years. This was part of the money we needed. We were short several thousand dollars and stressed over where we would find this money. We did not have anyone in the family who we would ask to borrow money from so my husband and I went to the credit union we dealt with from his work. We explained our situation with the top officer, who was also a friend of ours. He came up with a solution. Borrow the money and have it taken out of your pay. We already had an account with them for we had weekly deductions taken out of my husbands pay for a yearly vacation. The savings we already accumulated, plus the bonds we saved, left only a few thousand dollars needed. How fortunate that everything worked out. It told us that this house was meant to be.

The loan would be an added bill for a few years but without it we wouldn't be able to purchase the house. A brand new house...can you believe it! To save money on the mortgage, we did not add carpeting or appliances. So we had bare tiled floors and had to hand wash dishes and hang clothes to dry. I didn't care those items would be purchased one item at a time as we could afford them. The house was most important. I had nice areas, rugs for around the furniture in all rooms. They looked great in the apartment and would look even better in our home.

I immediately began packing items that weren't used often including clothing. I stacked up with nonperishable items in foods and cleaning products and stored them in brand new trash cans. All wall items and knick-knacks were down and packed My husband got promises from co-workers who were our friends to help us with the move. Things were falling into place and our dreams of owning our own house were about to become real.

What more could you want. We felt truly blessed and thankful to God for this big break.

Moving day came and so did the men, who promised to help us. By the time they had the truck with our belongings at our new home, other friends where there waiting to help us unload and get the house in order. The men moved the furniture into the moms as I explained where to put the pieces. Two of the women got into the cupboards, washed them and the dishes and then placed them into the cupboards where I thought would be the most practical for the everyday usage. I showed them which of the cupboards were to be used for dry goods and let them on their own. I in the meantime disinfected the bathrooms and all the floors as the men were done placing the furniture. Before you knew it the thick was empty and the house was completely furnished and all the odds and ends where finished.

What good friends we had. We never could have accomplished this much in one day if it weren't for them. Everything was so 01ganized and clean making the first night in our new home joyful. It was time to order pizza for everyone and crack open a few beers and sodas and celebrate. Everyone stayed for a couple of hours to relax and wish us well. It started to rain and immediately my one girlfriend spoke out to say, the rain will bring us luck not tears as in the old wives tale about a wedding with rain. We said our good byes and thanks to our friends and already planned our first get together. Our first night in our own home. How exciting and prideful we felt. How grateful we were, how a bit scared we felt about the new expense, but we were ready for the challenge. And I was right, the area rugs looked good in our house.

Our neighborhood was great. At the time we moved in their were just ten twin homes in our block. Five twins on each side of the street. The surrounding area was all empty lots and woods. The neighbors were all our age, some with children and a few waiting to have a family. We instantly became friends with all of them and took advantage of the summer weather and together sat out each evening getting to know one another better. Our two children were so happy to have new friends their age and played hard each day. We were in an ideal area. School was only our blocks away and the shopping was about the same in distance. What a convenient location we moved into.

Time to register the kids in school. How convenient to have a choice of schools within walking distance *from* our new home. We registered both of them in the same school as their new friends. They were excited and looked forward to going to school. We mothers took turns taking the younger children to kindergarten and picking them up afterwards. Our children became so close as did we adults. It was a happy neighborhood mainly because of our common ages and the fact we were equal in our economics. All of the husbands job incomes were just about the same and we wives woe stay at homes taking care of home, errands and children.

Years flew by and one by one we wives found the need to join the workforce. It seems once your child hits middle school, the school expenses gyt»vv and each of us had another child following the older ones footsteps. Sports and activities of all kind were added expenses. What to do...get a job, and we did. We were insistent to give our children more than what we grew up with. So employment for us was essential. Working, I believe helped us more than we expected. It opened additional horizons that we didn't even consider because we were so into raising our family.

What did working do for me? Having a position and earning an income gave me added confidence and the believability that I could do just about anything. I was a quick study and loved learning the techniques of business. I was very fortunate having supervisors, who were willing to train and teach me the methods of how their business was operating. Through the many years of my employment, and in each position I had, I was always able to advance to a higher rank. This is again thanks to the person, who took me under their guidance.

Entertainment was an early conversation that the neighborhood engaged in. We all agreed that since we were into a huge mortgage, had school expenses, etc., it would be great if we took turns having a get together in each of our homes. Great idea and we decided that no more than twice a month we would rotate houses for the get together The plan was each household would provide a dish and bring their own bottle and pmvicle a play mom for the kids. Sounds great doesn't it? And it worked for years. The secret for the successful get together was not to be pretentious. We liked and respected one another so much that we committed ourselves to be just who we were. Our genetic families grew close to our neighbors and their children as well. This made our neighborhood even mow special.

My life extends with my daughter and her husband, their two daughters, two great grandsons, my son and his spouse. My daughter lives on the same side of the block from me, just two twins away. My son lives fours blocks away. One grand daughter, and her family lives six hours away but we get to see them every few months. My other grand daughter lives an hour and a half from us and we see her often. I was blessed with the joy of having this family and I treasured those years of having them in my life more than words can describe. We are a close family and love one another deeply. I have said to my family since they woe a young age: "My heart is your heart...now and forever." These are words from my heart and soul.

When looking back, it's haul to believe that my lifetime has passed by so utterly fast. It seems unfair that after all the trials and tribulations of life, once concurred, your life is almost over. Why must we be cut offin life when now that all the challenges are settled and we can be of such importance to others, must our life end. H'm, it doesn't make sense to me.

I have often answered my friends when asked the question on life, 'do I believe decades have passed by, and where have they gone.' My answer is always that at times I felt life was sometimes my (beam of self Your young and living life as though it is forever, never realizing that indeed there is an end. Everything has it's end. I further explain that one night I went to sleep and when I woke up to a new day, my children were in their teens and in my late thirties. What happened to the first three decades? Still I again went to sleep and when I woke to a new rising sun, my children were grown, married and on their own. How frightening this reality was to me. Yet I again sleep for I must. When awake, only to find that now I am a woman in her seventies. I now have grown, adult grandchild and great grandchildren, all who are the love of my life. The days left of my life are numbered and there is still so much I wish to say and leave behind to their memories.

Is growing old fearful because of the fear of being alone? After all, your families are busy with their own lives. Does the fear of them not being wound in your old age sadden you? Is giving old dreadful because of the fear of being helpless and having to live in a home where you are given the care you will need? Yes, growing old is sad because you fear all these things and mostly because you fear the loss of your families love and thoughts of you. We all wish to be remembered with love and laughter

What do I leave behind for them other than things. I leave them with good memories of sharing time with them, tears of love and the joy of all those hugs and kisses. I leave them with written and verbal stories, and all those poems of life and experiences I was privileged to live. I leave them with my heart...now and forever

Helen Nastri